The BLACK PEARL PONIES series:

STORMCLOUD

JENNY OLDFIELD

Illustrated by
JOHN GREEN

*Hodder
Children's
Books*

A division of Hachette Children's Books

*Once more with thanks to the Foster family
and all my friends at Lost Valley Ranch, and this
time with special thanks to Katie Foster, horse
trainer and all-round equine expert.*

CHAPTER ONE

'Hey, Keira, take a look at this!' Josh Lucas invited his cousin to join him in the meadow at High Peak Ranch.

'Yeah, Keira – come and see!' Brooke urged.

Sisters Brooke and Keira were visiting High Peak with their dad. It was a Saturday morning in late April, with purple and white flowers in the fresh green grass and snow still clinging to the mountain peaks under a sky of forget-me-not blue.

1

Keira tore herself away from the day-old foal in the barn and ran across the corral to join Josh and Brooke. 'I'll be back,' she promised the mom – a pretty sorrel mare who was fussing over her groggy newborn.

She reached the meadow gate and climbed up to sit next to Josh. 'What am I looking at?' she asked.

'This!' he said, pointing to a colt in the meadow.

The young horse was a dark dappled grey with a jet black mane and tail. He looked undersized, with a saddle strapped to his back and a guy about to set his cowboy boot in the stirrup. The guy was Kevin Lucas, Josh's dad.

Keira focused on the colt who was sidestepping

away from her uncle and laying his ears flat. 'It doesn't look like he's been ridden much,' she muttered.

'He's not happy,' Brooke agreed. The girls frowned as the pony took the weight of his rider and started to crow hop across the meadow.

'What's his name?' Keira wanted to know.

'We named him Stormcloud – Stormy for short.' Anxiously, Josh held the top bar of the gate with both hands. He gripped so hard, his knuckles were white. 'Dad bought him from the sale barn at Elk Springs.'

'Whoa, look at that!' Brooke gasped.

With Kevin on his back, Stormcloud had gone from crow hopping to serious bucking. He arched his back and jumped straight up in the air, head down and mane flying. He landed and bucked again – twice then three times.

Kevin sat deep in the saddle and went with the rough ride. He held Stormy on a tight rein, sitting back in the saddle, legs straight forward. Then, the second the colt landed and jerked him forward, he lurched with him, bending his knees and tucking his feet well back.

'Your dad's a great rider,' Brooke murmured, holding her breath as Stormcloud changed tactics and began to rear. Up he went on his hind legs, front hooves pawing the air.

Keira watched him flare his nostrils and curl his lip to show his teeth. His eyes were rolling in his head. 'That pony is so not happy!' she sighed.

Stormy went on rearing, trying to tip his rider backwards out of the saddle. Then he went back to bucking, twisting his whole body as he landed, flinging Kevin from this side to that until at last the reins were whipped out of the rider's hands and Kevin was thrown sideways on to the ground.

'Whoa!' Brooke gasped. She and Josh jumped down from the gate and sprinted across the meadow to help Kevin. Meanwhile, Stormcloud grabbed his chance of freedom and galloped away.

'How about that?' a calm voice said at Keira's shoulder.

She turned to find that her dad had been right there, quietly viewing Stormy's antics. 'It wasn't good to watch.' Keira hated to see a horse unhappy with its rider, getting its mouth tugged and hurt by the metal bit.

'Stormy sure doesn't know much about being a

saddle horse,' Jacob agreed. 'Which won't come as any surprise to Kevin, to tell you the truth.'

Still frowning, Keira climbed down from the gate. She saw Josh and Brooke help Kevin to his feet while Stormcloud galloped to the far fence and stood, sides heaving, head raised and neighing shrilly. 'So where did Uncle Kevin find Stormy?' she asked her dad.

'He came straight off the rodeo circuit,' Jacob told her. 'My soft-hearted brother spotted him at the local sale barn and felt sorry for him, I guess.'

'He's a rodeo pony?' Keira checked. In the distance Stormcloud set off again at a gallop, dragging his reins along the ground, zigzagging across the meadow until he reached a fence, then he turned and galloped again. He seemed to be running, running, running with nowhere to go. 'Poor guy,' Keira sighed.

'Kevin's heart ruled his head like it usually does,' Jacob muttered, watching Stormy with an expert horse trainer's eye. 'You can't go spending hard-earned cash on a colt because you feel sorry for him, then when you get him home you find you can't even step in the saddle without him bucking and rearing.'

'But you can't blame Stormy,' Keira argued. Her own heart went out to the rodeo pony still galloping rider-less across the meadow as Josh and Brooke helped Kevin towards the gate. 'Not if he spent his whole life at the rodeo. Think about it – bucking his rider out of the saddle is all he knows.'

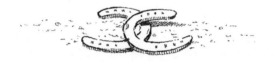

Back in the barn, Keira eased open the door of the stall where the newborn foal slept in a bed of clean straw. She crouched beside the baby and reached out to touch his warm, fuzzy mane. 'So soft!' she whispered.

The foal's mom hovered nearby, snickering gently.

'Go ahead – stroke him,' Josh encouraged. 'Dad likes us to handle the foals from day one – it gets them used to the idea that we humans are on the same side, not aliens from a different planet.'

'So-o-o pretty!' Keira breathed.

The foal lay with his gangly, stick-like legs folded under him, eyes closed and breathing evenly. His head seemed too big for his skinny, nut-brown body.

'It's a technique Dad learned at veterinary school,' Josh went on as he watched Keira handle the foal. 'It's called imprinting. They reckon you have to handle the foals as often as you can – all the way along the spine, and especially around the head and neck area.'

'So how is your dad?' Keira asked. She glanced up at the sorrel mare who was rustling through the straw towards her. 'Hey, you want to be with your

baby?' she murmured, moving out of the way to let the mare in.

The mom nuzzled at her sleeping baby, roused him and gave him time to struggle to his feet and start to suckle.

'Dad's cool – no bones broken. Only his pride took a knock,' Josh grinned. 'Especially when he knew Uncle Jacob had been watching.'

'And how about Stormcloud?' Keira asked. The last she'd seen, Stormy had been cornered by Brooke and Jacob in a far corner of the meadow. 'Did they get close enough to grab his reins?'

Josh nodded. 'They took off his saddle and left him to chill out. You want to take another look?'

'Sure.' Keira tore herself away from the contented mare and foal and walked with Josh across the corral back to the meadow fence where they found the grey colt quietly grazing.

'He looks happy now.' Keira admired the dappled markings on Stormy's back. His black mane and tail gleamed in the sunlight.

'We need to let him eat,' Josh commented. Keira's eleven-year-old cousin was a vet's son and he already knew plenty about pony welfare. 'The day we got him home from the sale barn we knew he was a poor keeper. Plus, he doesn't know how to roll on the ground to relax – how about that?'

'I feel sorry for him,' Keira sighed. 'Did Uncle Kevin buy him from the JLK Barn?'

Josh shook his head. 'Nope. The guys at JLK take good care of their stock before they sell them on. Dad was passing by a run-down place outside of Elk Springs when he saw some rodeo guys leading Stormy out of a trailer. The poor little guy was covered in dirt, his mane was knotted and his ribs showed so bad you could have played a tune on them.'

'Poor Stormy,' Keira sighed again. 'You know my dad – the second he spots an animal in need of help, he moves right in,' said Josh. 'So he pulls up his trailer, walks into that barn and waits for this one to come up for auction. Stormy looked so bad no one else even put in a bid. Dad bought him at a bargain-basement price.'

'Cool,' Keira murmured.

The cousins watched as Stormcloud raised his head and listened to the sound of the wind in the pine trees beyond the meadow. To Keira he still seemed to be scenting the freedom he'd been looking for when he galloped aimlessly around the meadow.

'Yeah, but now we have a big problem,' Josh pointed out.

Guessing what was coming, Keira's heart missed a beat. 'Uncle Kevin bought a pony that no one can use?'

Josh nodded. 'Once a rodeo pony, always a

15

rodeo pony,' he muttered. 'No one's ever going to ride that bucking bronco, no matter how good a rider they think they are.'

CHAPTER TWO

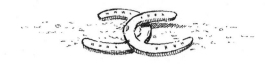

That night the temperature fell below zero and an early morning frost brought Popcorn, the Black Pearl ginger cat, into the warm kitchen where he snuck on to Brooke's lap.

'Hey, don't get too cosy,' Brooke smiled as she stroked him and tickled his chin. 'I have chores to do!'

Miaow! Popcorn ignored her and snuggled down.

'Where's today's list of chores?' Keira asked, yawning as she came downstairs and into the kitchen.

'On top of my magazine,' her mom told her. Allyson was cooking the usual ranch breakfast of bacon and eggs over easy, serving it up on slices of warm wheat toast.

Sleepily, Keira took the slip of paper from her mom's copy of Western Magazine, glancing at the open page before she ran through the items on the list. "Quality. Fit. Style." she read in a full page ad for classic cowboy boots. The picture showed a pair of beautiful, tooled jersey-calf boots under a well-known brand name and a logo that read "Exclusive since 1883". 'Nice boots,' she murmured.

'And way out of my price range,' Allyson sighed,

 glancing at her own pair of worn boots by the kitchen door. 'Still, a girl can dream!'

'Come on, Keira, read the list,' Brooke urged, biting into her toasted sandwich.

'Number one – poop-scoop and rake the round pen,' Keira began slowly, still feeling sorry about the worn-down heels, cracked leather uppers and turned-up toes of her mom's old boots. They were the only ones she owned and, since money was always tight at Black Pearl Ranch, the boots would have to be worn at all the top-class reining competitions Allyson had entered for the spring and summer. 'Number two – saddle up Nemo ready for Dad . . .'

Sighing, Brooke lifted Popcorn from her lap and put him on the floor. 'You scoop and rake, I'll saddle,' she decided and she headed outside before Keira could argue.

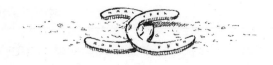

Keira was scooping poop in the round pen and raking the soft dirt surface when her mom finished clearing away breakfast plates and came to help.

'Good job,' Allyson told Keira, seizing another rake and joining her. 'So tell me about Uncle Kevin's accident. Your dad says he was lucky to come out with just a few bruises.'

'Yeah – Stormcloud thought he was still at the

rodeo,' Keira told her. 'He bucked him off real good.' And she explained what Josh had told her about the colt's history and how he ended his short career unwanted at the sale barn.

Allyson raked and listened. 'What can you do?' she sighed. 'You can't leave him there to be sent for dog food.'

'Yuck – don't think about it!' Keira shuddered. 'But now Josh says they don't know what to do with Stormy. If they can't ride him, what kind of future does he have at High Peak?'

Allyson nodded. 'I hear you. They're short of cash, the way we are here at Black Pearl, especially since Aunty Lori went off to California to study for her veterinarian degree.'

'But they'll be good when she finishes her

training.' Keira knew that having two vets in the family would double their income. Meanwhile her own family scraped by on whatever her dad could earn from horse training and on the prize money her mom won in competitions. And that's the way it would be until she and Brooke were old enough to get paid for working

alongside their dad.

'Still,' Allyson said as she opened the gate to let Brooke ride Nemo into the round pen, followed by Jacob on foot.

The little Palomino came in eager to work, trotting around the pen with his head held high. 'Right now Kevin and Josh have a colt they can't handle. And these days who can afford to keep stock just out of the goodness of their heart?'

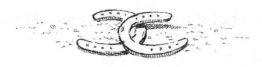

For a while Keira forgot about the problem of Stormcloud the bucking bronco. Instead, she got wrapped up in watching Brooke work with Nemo, listening to her dad give instructions to horse and rider.

'Always react to what your pony is telling you,' he called. 'If Nemo acts up every time he passes by the gate, try to work out what he doesn't like. Is it the sack of grain pellets leaning against the fence, or is it that saddle pad slung over the rail?'

'Something's spooking him for sure,' Brooke agreed. 'I guess it's the way the pad is flapping in the breeze.'

Keira watched Nemo cock an ear and step suddenly away from the saddle pad towards the centre of the pen. Brooke corrected him and kept him trotting on. Nemo was a cute pony with beautiful Palomino colouring – the honey-brown coat and pale blonde mane and tail – a poster pony for every horse-loving kid's bedroom wall.

'Good – use your leg to steer him back on course,' Jacob called. 'Neck rein him to the left at the same time – good job!'

'When do Nemo's owners come to collect him?' Keira asked Allyson.

'Next Saturday. The Forresters aim to have their daughter Cindy riding him in the junior reining contest on May 1st.'

'At Elk Springs?' Keira queried. She'd entered herself and Red Star into the same competition.

'That's the one. Nemo should do great.'

'That's because he's had the best trainer!' Keira grinned. She knew how hard her dad worked on the bond between pony and rider. At Black Pearl Ranch they never used force or cruelty – just straightforward respect and friendship. The results proved that his method worked better than any others and Jacob Lucas's reputation as a trainer rose every time one of his ponies got placed in county competitions.

'Which means I need to get to work with Red Star right away if we aim to win on May 1st,' she added, putting down the rake and making for the barn.

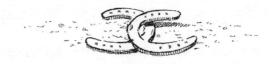

Keira and Red Star began training as soon as Brooke and Jacob finished with Nemo. They crossed paths in the corral – Nemo tossed his pale mane and gave Red Star a neigh of greeting as if he was saying, *Your turn now!*

Red Star neighed back cheekily. *Stick around and watch me!* He strutted into the pen, ready to show the Palomino how sliding stops were really done.

'OK, let's go!' Keira murmured, putting her

strawberry roan pony into a lope across the centre of the pen. As they neared the far fence, she reined him back and made him lower his hind quarters so that his front legs were braced and his back feet skidded to a halt. They stopped just a metre short of the fence.

'Nice work,' Allyson said from the gate. 'Carry on working on stops for ten minutes then switch to flying lead changes. I'll be back in fifteen.'

For Keira, her time in the pen with Red Star was always the best part of the day. In time, she hoped to follow in her mom's footsteps, becoming adult county champion for three years running. For now, she just lived and loved every lead change, every switch from walk to lope to gallop. 'Good boy!' she breathed, leaning forward to pat

Red Star's neck. Then, 'Good job!' as he perfected his sliding stop. 'Watch out, Nemo – see you at Elk Springs!'

CHAPTER THREE

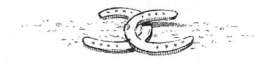

The sun was up and gaining heat and the sky crystal clear when Keira's mom came back as promised. Keira saw her cross the corral and so she pulled up at the gate. 'How did we look?' she asked.

'Good, but still room for improvement.' Allyson was tough to please when it came to horsemanship.

Proud Red Star tossed his mane from his face and stamped impatiently. *What do you mean – room for improvement?*

Keira and her mom laughed. 'Fifteen more minutes and then finish,' Allyson advised. 'Then you can brush him down and put him out in the meadow with Annie and Misty. After that it's my turn – I plan to work with Captain for half an hour.'

'Can I watch?' Keira asked, hoping, as always, to pick up tips.

Allyson nodded. 'When we're through in the round pen there's somewhere I have to be. I thought maybe you'd like to come along for the ride.'

'OK,' Keira quickly agreed. 'Where are we going?'

'High Peak Ranch. Yesterday your dad forgot to take the new chaps he made for Josh,' Allyson said. 'We'll take a ride back there and you can show me that bucking bronco they bought by mistake – that's if you'd like to.'

Keira searched her mom's face for an unspoken message. Yes, there was a twinkle in her eye and a twitch at the corners of her mouth – it was really Allyson who wanted to sneak a look at the bronco. 'You betcha!' Keira cried eagerly. 'I'll call Josh and tell him we're on our way!'

'Could Josh be right?' Keira asked as Allyson drove the winding road up into the mountains. She was staring thoughtfully out of the window at a herd of mule deer grazing on a hilltop beneath a stand of aspens. 'He said that no one can ever ride Stormy, no matter how good a rider they are?'

Her mom took a while to answer. 'I guess he

means, you can take a pony out of the rodeo but you can't take the rodeo out of a pony.'

'Huh?' Keira didn't get it.

'The ways of the rodeo are bred into ponies like Stormcloud,' Allyson explained. 'The mare who gave birth to him and the stallion who fathered him will have been rodeo stock themselves, and they were most likely bred in the wild, out somewhere in the Californian desert. Genetically, Stormy is programmed to run – to take flight – and when he's trapped and has a saddle thrown over his back, his instinct is to buck and carry on bucking until he plumb wears himself out!'

'I hear you,' Keira sighed.

Her mom glanced sideways at her. 'But you don't believe me?'

33

'Yeah – no – I don't know!' Keira wanted to believe that every pony on the planet would respond to the training they did at Black Pearl Ranch. But then she remembered the way Stormy had acted in the meadow with her uncle Kevin, and she had to allow that the genetic theory might be correct.

Her mom turned up the dirt track to High Peak and the truck rattled over the iron cattle guard. 'Me neither,' she admitted. 'I don't know what to think. It's down to breeding *and* training, I guess, and until you test it out you just don't know which will turn out stronger.'

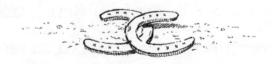

Once Keira and Allyson pulled up outside the

house at High Peak, there was no more time to puzzle out an answer.

'Here are your chaps,' Allyson told Kevin, who had limped on to the porch to greet them. 'Jacob says he's sorry he forgot to bring them yesterday.'

Keira's uncle took the leather chaps and admired the engraved silver buckle, fancy fringing and scalloped edges. 'Nice job,' he grinned. 'How much do I owe him?'

Allyson shook her head. 'Hey, you're family.'

'But I still want to pay.'

'No way,' Keira's mom insisted. 'I hear you took a fall. How's your leg?'

'Bruised, but nothing serious.' Kevin made light of his injury and led them across the corral to the tack room where he hung the chaps on the porch rail. 'I thought we'd find Josh here,' he told Keira, 'but it looks like he took a saddle from the rack . . .'

'There he is!' Keira had heard hooves galloping across the meadow and turned to see Josh riding hell for leather towards the gate. He was on Stormcloud, his legs were out of the stirrups and his reins were flying loose.

'Watch out!' Josh yelled as he saw his dad step

down from the porch. 'This bronco is out of control!'

Sure enough, Stormy charged at the meadow gate and when he came to within a couple of strides, he leaned back on his haunches and took off.

'Look at that – he jumped clean over!' Keira gasped.

The pony's hooves hit the dirt surface of the corral and he galloped on. By now, Josh had thrown himself forward and was clinging to Stormy's neck. They charged past Kevin, Keira and Allyson, close enough for them to see that his ears lay flat and his nostrils were flared wide. Specks of white froth had gathered at the corners of his mouth.

'Jump clear!' Kevin yelled at his son. 'Now, Josh!'

Stormcloud had crossed the corral and was out through the open gate on to the dirt track. He veered downhill towards a creek that ran through the valley. Beyond the creek was a stand of willows and beyond that, rising steeply, were the foothills of High Peak.

'Jump!' Kevin and Allyson yelled again.

The pony surged into the clear water, raising spray and galloping on. Listening to the advice, Josh relaxed his grip and slid from Stormy's back into the water, which softened his fall. He landed waist deep, staggered backwards and sat down in the creek. Meanwhile, Stormcloud made the far bank and ran on.

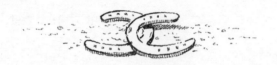

'What were you thinking?' Kevin demanded as Allyson and Keira ran to help Josh up the bank.

Josh was dripping wet and held his left wrist to his chest. He hung his head as he faced his dad.

'Yeah – what did you tell me yesterday?' Keira reminded him. 'No one is ever going to ride a bucking bronco, no matter how good they think they are!'

'I know, I know,' Josh groaned. 'But it was bugging me. I just thought maybe I could prove myself wrong!'

'Idiot!' Kevin muttered, but Keira could see her uncle was relieved that Josh hadn't done himself serious damage. 'You need to get out of those wet clothes and let me take a look at that wrist.'

Keira and Allyson watched Kevin lead Josh inside, then Allyson nodded towards their truck. 'Let's drive up the track, see if we can find Stormy's trail,' she suggested.

So they set off along the rough road, heading wide of the willows and up the steep hill, looking out for the grey colt but seeing only mule deer standing alert and silent under the tall pine trees.

'He could be anywhere,' Allyson murmured, stopping the truck and stepping out to scan the rocky hillside. 'He could take cover down any of these narrow draws, between the trees or behind the boulders.'

Keira agreed. Though the sun was shining, she shivered in the cold breeze and saw that they'd

41

almost reached the snow line where the trees stopped growing and the snow lingered even this late in the year. 'He wouldn't go up into the snow drifts, would he?' she asked.

'I don't reckon he would.' Allyson set off on foot towards the nearest steep gulley, crouching down to examine the ground then calling Keira across. 'Hoof marks,' she pointed out.

Keira made out the direction of the prints and she and her mom followed them deeper into the gulley. Close to an almost vertical rock face, Allyson raised her finger to her lips.

Keira held her breath and listened. There was no single sound she could make out, only a living, breathing sense that there was an animal nearby.

Her mom pointed deeper into the draw and they

crept forward. They
reached the end of
the rock face and
turned a corner.

There, in a dead
end where more cliffs
converged, Stormcloud
stood. He faced them head on, flesh quivering and
nostrils flared wide, showing the whites of his eyes.

'It's OK,' Keira whispered. 'We won't harm you.'

Stormy fixed them with his gaze, watched them
take one, two, three steps towards him. Then he
exploded. Up he went on his hind legs, pawing the
air, bringing his front hooves crashing down on to
the stony ground. Up again, striking out with his
hooves, thudding down only metres away. A third

time he reared, neighing out a shrill warning.

With split second timing Allyson grabbed Keira's wrist and pulled her to one side.

Stormy reared and came down, saw an opening and charged through. They saw the whites of those frightened eyes, felt the lash of his black tail as he thundered by.

There was nothing Keira and Allyson could do, except stand in that dead end and watch Stormcloud run.

CHAPTER FOUR

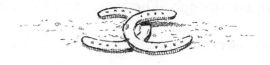

All that night Keira worried about the runaway pony. She went to sleep worrying about him and woke up with the same heavy feeling – a fear that something really bad would happen up there on High Peak.

But Monday was a home-school day for her and Brooke and by nine o'clock, Allyson had them both concentrating on maths problems while she helped Jacob work with Nemo in the round pen.

Keira sat for a full hour over her page of figures. She stared so hard that the numbers seemed to float and she found she couldn't come up with any

 answers. When her mom came back into the house, she saw that Keira's mind was on other things.

'It's Stormcloud, isn't it?' Allyson asked.

Keira nodded. 'It fell way below zero last night, and if Stormy was lost on the mountain he could freeze to death.'

'Wait – I'll call Kevin, see if they have any news.' Allyson picked up the phone, spoke for a while then ended the conversation and shook her head.

'Nothing,' she reported. 'So, Keira, why don't you leave your school work for a while and get involved in something practical?'

'Like what?' Keira sighed. *Poor Stormy – still out on High Peak, lost and lonesome.*

'Like working with Red Star,' Allyson suggested. 'It'll take your mind off the runaway pony. Besides, your dad has just about finished his training session with Nemo.'

Keira didn't need telling twice. She flung down her pen and ran outside, pausing only to shove her feet into her cowboy boots which stood in line beside her mom's and Brooke's on the porch. Five minutes later, she'd saddled Red Star and was heading for the pen.

Jacob stood at the gate with Nemo. He held it

open to let Keira ride in. 'What is it this morning –
flying lead changes?' he asked.

'Nope. We need to work on spins for Elk
Springs,' she told him. 'Both clockwise and anti-
clockwise. How did Nemo do?'

'OK,' Jacob said with a frown.

'Only OK?'

'Yeah. His heart wasn't in it this morning, so I
plan to give him the rest of the day off.' Shaking his
head, Jacob led the little Palomino into the corral.

Meanwhile, Keira got to work on Red Star. She
rode him to the centre of the pen, halted then neck-
reined him to the right, sitting well back in the
saddle and applying pressure with her left leg. Red
Star went straight into a rapid clockwise spin,
crossing his front feet as delicately as a dancer,

staying fixed to the spot on his hind legs. He spun until Keira eased the pressure.

'Good job!' she breathed, leaning forward to pat his neck.

He lifted his head and pranced a little. *What next?* Then suddenly, something on the hillside caught his attention and he stood stock still, ears pricked.

'What?' Keira asked, looking in the same direction and seeing nothing.

Red Star tilted his head back, opened his mouth and neighed loudly.

From way up the wooded slope he received an answer – a high, frightened whinny.

Red Star called a second time. Again the answer came back.

'Who's that?' Keira muttered. At first she thought that one of the Black Pearl ponies had escaped. She rode quickly out of the round pen, across the corral to the meadow to check. No, they were all there, including Nemo, who stood unhappily by the gate just gazing across at Captain, Misty, Annie and the brood mares, Willow and Ruby. So who was calling from the hillside?

'Come on, Red Star, let's take a look,' she decided.

Without stopping to tell Jacob, she trotted her pony along the Jeep trail up to Dolphin Rock, where she stopped at the cattle guard to let Red Star call again. She sat in the saddle searching the slopes, looking for any sign of movement. For ages she saw nothing until, there, among the pine trees above the smooth, flattened dome of Dolphin Rock, something stirred.

'Let's go,' she whispered to Red Star and urged him on.

Red Star snorted and began to pick his way between the trees. Beneath his hooves twigs cracked and snapped. A black squirrel crossed their path and shot straight up a tree trunk.

On they headed until they reached the crest of the hill and looked over the ridge down into the next valley where Sharman Lake glittered in the sun. Keira reined Red Star back. 'I guess we lost the trail,' she sighed.

But her pony tossed his head and seemed determined to walk on along the ridge until he reached some tall fingers of rock which cast a deep shadow. It was here that Red Star slowed down.

'Did you see something?' Keira whispered.

His ears flicked; he listened hard.

Crack! A twig snapped. Then there was the

hollow sound of hooves on hard rock and the first glimpse of a large creature moving out of the shadows – a grey, silent shape . . . a strong, broad back, a tangled black mane.

'Stormcloud!' Keira gasped.

The runaway pony approached warily. His dappled coat was covered in dust and prickly burrs were tangled in his tail. Keira noticed that his saddle was missing – somehow along the way the cinch must have snapped and the saddle had slid to the ground. But his bridle was in place and his reins trailed in the dust.

'Poor boy, we won't hurt you!' Keira breathed. 'You're tired and hungry, and real scared – I know how you feel. Look at Red Star – see how glad he is to see you!'

Red Star had lowered his head and was licking his lips – a sure sign that he wanted to be friends. He let Stormy come right up to him and then he stretched his neck and rubbed his nose against Stormy's withers.

'Me too,' Keira murmured, reaching out slowly and smoothly to pick up one of the trailing reins. 'I'm so-o-o glad you chose to head for Black Pearl Ranch!'

Red Star snorted and pawed the dusty ground. He turned for home.

Keira gave a gentle tug on the rein. 'C'mon, Stormy – come with us!'

For a second the runaway rodeo pony dug in his heels and tugged backwards.

Red Star waited and snorted a second time. Keira

tugged again. 'We'll give you feed and water,' she promised. 'We'll let you rest up then we'll call Josh and Uncle Kevin.'

Gradually, Red Star's friendly snorts and Keira's gentle voice soothed Stormcloud. He stopped pulling and took a step forwards, then another.

'Good boy!' Keira held on to Stormy's rein and led him down from the ridge. She felt relief flood through her. 'This is going to work out,' she murmured. 'Everything will be totally fine. Just you wait and see!'

CHAPTER FIVE

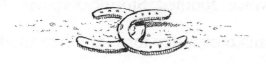

Jacob stood on the tack room porch, watching Keira and Red Star lead Stormcloud to safety.

They came slowly along the Jeep trail under the high noon sun, taking their time, waiting for the weary runaway to get used to the idea of coming back into civilisation.

'Good job, honey!' Jacob called as Keira brought Stormy safely into the corral. He kicked into action, taking Stormy's rein from her and leading him straight to the water tub beside the barn door. 'Give me the details later. First we have to get this guy fed and watered.'

'Pellets?' she checked, jumping out of the saddle and slipping a headstall on to Red Star so she could tether him to the rail.

'Two scoops,' her dad told her. He ran his hands along Stormy's back and up and down his legs, checking for injuries.

Inside the barn, Keira poured grain pellets into a bucket and ran back to the corral. She waited until Stormy had finished sucking up water then offered him the feed. Soon he had his head in the bucket and was munching happily.

'So?' Jacob said to Keira, standing back with his arms folded. 'What's the story, morning glory?'

'It was like this,' Jacob told his brother over the phone. 'Keira was working with Red Star when she heard Stormy calling down the hillside . . . '

'Actually, it was Red Star who heard him first,' Keira whispered to Brooke. 'He was the real hero.'

' . . . Josh found his saddle under a tree by the creek?' Jacob was echoing.

'Stormy only agreed to come back with us because Red Star persuaded him,' Keira told Allyson. 'Remember how it was when we tried to get near him?'

'No way would he come with us,' Allyson agreed. 'But it does sound like he decided to trust Red Star.'

'So what do you want us to do with him now?' Jacob asked Kevin. As he listened to the answer, a frown appeared on his face. 'Don't you need to think about this a while?' he asked.

Keira, Brooke and Allyson tuned into the one-sided conversation, trying to work out what was going on. Jacob had begun to shake his head.

'Maybe Uncle Kevin wants to send Stormy back to the sale barn,' Brooke suggested in a whisper.

'No, he can't do that!' Keira remembered the last time it had happened, when nobody except her uncle had put in a bid. And she knew what happened to ponies that no one wanted.

'Sshh!' Allyson warned.

At last Jacob came off the phone. He chewed his lip thoughtfully.

'So?' Allyson asked. Keira put her hands to her ears, hardly able to listen.

'Kevin doesn't want us to take Stormcloud back to High Peak,' he explained.

No, don't say it. Don't let him get sold again! Keira pleaded silently. She was almost at the point of running out and unbolting the corral gate to let Stormy run free a second time. Anything – a lonely life on the mountain, battling the weather and foraging for food – anything was better than the sale barn!

'He said we could keep him,' Jacob went on. 'Kevin's exact words were, "If you can retrain that bronco and make something of him, you're welcome to sell him on to a decent owner and keep the profit."'

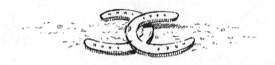

'"If!"' Allyson stressed the most important word in Kevin Lucas's sentence.

The family had gathered on the porch after lunch to discuss the offer. 'If we can retrain Stormy . . .'

'Should we even try?' Jacob wondered. From here they had a good view of the runaway rodeo pony, who stood quietly with Red Star in the cool shadow cast by the barn. 'We already know that he bucks and rears. He hates a saddle on his back, plus he spooks and runs. For all we know, you could add kicking, nipping and biting to an already long list of bad habits.'

'It's a big challenge,' Allyson admitted.

'And I don't have the time right now,' Jacob went

on. 'As soon as I finish working with Nemo, I get three new colts to train for the dude ranch out at Sharman. They want those ponies on the guest string by fall this year. That's a lot of work to get them ready.'

'And I have to focus on competing,' Allyson said reluctantly. 'Springtime and early summer is when most of the competitions fall. And this year we really need that prize money.'

Listening to her mom and dad, Keira's heart, which had been soaring when she first heard her uncle's offer, sank again. *We have to keep Stormy!* she thought. *Without us, he doesn't have any kind of life to look forward to!*

Brooke was the one who broke the heavy silence. She looked her sister straight in the eye. 'Keira, maybe you can find the time?' she said quietly.

Me? Keira opened her eyes wide, took two seconds to let the idea take root. Then, 'Yes!' she cried. 'Of course – me!'

Brooke smiled and nodded.

'What do you think?' Jacob asked Allyson, his expression guarded.

Keira's mom studied the dappled grey bronco in the corral. 'Like I said, it's a big challenge – there's no denying it. But there's money in it for you, Keira, if you do a good job.'

'I can do it!' Keira insisted. The money didn't matter – Stormy's life was at stake here!

'So, it's worth a try,' Jacob agreed cautiously. He nodded briefly and walked back into the house, hands in pockets.

'Don't worry – I'll talk to him,' Allyson said, following him inside.

Keira turned to Brooke with a big smile. 'Thanks,' she breathed. 'That was a cool idea.'

Brooke grinned back. 'This is the first pony you get to train and sell by yourself, thanks to Uncle Kevin.'

'I know – so-o-o cool!' Keira sighed as she stared out at Stormcloud standing good as gold next to Red Star. She leaned on the porch rail, letting her gaze range over the flaking paint on the barn door, the worn saddle pads slung over the corral fence and allowing it to come to rest on the row of boots by the door. 'And I know just what I'm going to do with the money!' she said with a big bright smile.

CHAPTER SIX

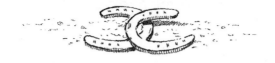

Day one of Stormy's training started in the meadow, amongst the blue columbines and white chickweed growing up through the fresh green grass.

'We're not even going to go into the round pen,' Keira reported to Jacob, Allyson and Brooke as she left the house soon after breakfast on Tuesday morning. 'I plan to put a headstall on him and work him on a long line out by the creek.'

'Sounds good to me,' her mom agreed, clearing the breakfast plates.

'Me too.' Jacob reached for his Stetson and headed out on to the porch with Keira. 'Slow and easy does it with Stormcloud. Anyhow, I'll be using the pen with Nemo, trying to sort out a couple of issues he's developed lately.'

'See you later!' Keira called. She collected a headstall and long lunge rein from the tack room and ran to the meadow where she greeted Red Star, who trotted to the gate for his good-morning nose rub. 'Hey!' she murmured, balling her hand and kneading Red Star's nose with her knuckles. 'How's your new buddy?'

From across the meadow, Stormcloud looked towards Keira and Red Star. He kept a wary distance from Misty and Annie, staying close to the two brood mares who were drinking from the creek.

'You settled in OK?' Keira asked, walking towards him with Red Star at her side, the rope and halter looped over her shoulder. 'Did you get to know Ruby and Willow? They're about to have babies any day now.'

Stormy's head was up, his ears flicked forwards, alert and suspicious. Keira kept on talking. 'Today is the day you learn to roll,' she announced, approaching slowly with her eyes cast downwards to avoid direct contact with Stormy. 'Rolling is so much fun,' she went on. 'Sure. It's scary at first – you're down on the ground with your feet in the air and who knows what's going to jump out of the

bushes and grab you? But listen to me – you get to rub your back in the grass, which feels great. Then you roll right over and shake yourself down. Red Star will show you how.'

Turning to Red Star, Keira gave him the command to roll and her well-trained pony sank to his knees. Over on his side he went, squirming with pleasure as he made contact with the cool grass.

'All the way over!' Keira told him.

He squirmed some more then kicked, throwing his weight sideways so that he turned on to his back where he wriggled and waved his legs in the air.

'And up again,' Keira encouraged.

Another sideways kick and Red Star had rolled right over, bent his knees under him and stood up. He gave Stormy a look that said, *see – nothing to it!*

'Now it's your turn,' Keira told him softly, crouching down and slipping her hand in her pocket to pull out a juicy red apple. 'You need to kneel to reach this, OK?'

Tempted by the apple, Stormy went down on his knees. Keira moved the treat sideways and lower still. 'Come on to your side.' He stretched his neck and collapsed on to his side. 'Feels good, doesn't

71

it?' she whispered. 'How about the full works – the roll on to your back to see how cool that is?'

Stormy lay on his side. He squirmed a little.

'No one's going to come and get you,' Keira cooed. 'Good boy – over you go.'

Slowly, Stormy kicked his legs and heaved himself over in the ungainly way that ponies have. He was on his back, legs in the air and enjoying the cool grass, wriggling happily.

'Good boy!' Keira tempted him over with the apple, moving it just out of reach until he rolled again, bent his knees under him and stood up. 'You so deserve this!' she sighed, offering him the apple on the palm of her hand.

Stormcloud took it between his big front teeth. Crunch! The apple vanished.

'Life's pretty good, huh?' Keira grinned as Stormy munched, standing in a meadow full of flowers by a crystal-clear creek under a pure blue sky.

'I got him to roll and then he let me put on the headstall and long rein him by the creek,' Keira announced at lunch. 'I guess that's enough for today.'

'Good – you went right back to the beginning with him,' Allyson encouraged. 'I reckon it'll be a while before you put a saddle back on him though.'

'Talking of which,' Jacob broke in. 'I just spoke to my brother and he says he'll bring Stormy's saddle with him when he visits later today.'

'What brings Kevin back to Black Pearl so soon?' Allyson asked as she got ready to work with Captain on their reining competition routine.

'I asked him to come.' Jacob finished his sandwich then took a long swig of iced water. 'I want him to take a look at Nemo.'

'Is there a problem?' Keira's mom looked suddenly worried.

'Maybe, maybe not.' Jacob shrugged. 'It's something I need a vet's opinion on before I mention it to the owners.'

'OK, we'll worry about it later,' Allyson decided, turning to Brooke and Keira and telling them to log on to their computers before she gave them their science tasks for the afternoon.

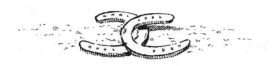

It was late in the evening and the sun was setting over the Black Pearl range before Kevin and Josh made it to the ranch.

'Sorry we're late,' Kevin said as he lifted Stormy's heavy saddle from the back of his truck. 'I had to stop by Tom Walters' place to check on a couple of pregnant cattle.'

Josh took the saddle from his dad, ready to carry it into the tack room. 'You'll need a new cinch,' he explained to Keira. 'The old one snapped while Stormy was on the run.'

'No problem.' Keira told Josh about her progress so far. 'Tomorrow I'll do more with him on the long line, and this time I'll take him into the round pen.'

The cousins were still discussing Stormy when Jacob and Kevin joined them in the corral.

'I sent Brooke to bring Nemo in from the meadow,' Jacob told his brother. 'There's something about his trot that isn't right – he's kind of off-balance. I'm hoping you can tell me if there's a serious problem.'

Kevin nodded and waited for Brooke to reappear with the little Palomino. 'Can you trot him by me?' he asked Brooke, who ran the pony across the corral so that her uncle could take a good look. 'OK, thanks.' Kevin strode across and Brooke held Nemo while Kevin lifted his right front foot. He ran his hand up and down the leg, noticing when the pony reacted to his touch.

'Anything?' Jacob asked.

'No swelling,' Kevin muttered as he continued his investigation. 'But he's favouring the other leg for sure, and he's feeling some pain right here.'

'Is it down in the pedal bone?' Jacob was frowning and bending down beside Kevin. They went on discussing Nemo's problem in low voices.

'They call that the coffin bone too,' Josh told Brooke and Keira. He was easy to read, like his dad – and he looked like him too, with his curly brown hair and freckled face. Right now he looked worried. 'You crack that pedal bone and the pony is out of action for months.'

'And Dad is the one who'll have to tell the Forresters,' Brooke sighed.

'Cindy will miss the competition at Elk Springs,' Keira realised.

'Unless Nemo comes good before Saturday,' Brooke said. 'That's when Cindy and her mom come to pick him up.'

They held their breaths and waited for Kevin to finish his examination. 'This needs an X-ray,' he decided.

'So I have to call the owners.' Jacob stood up and crossed his arms over his chest, looking up at the sun sinking behind the mountain. 'If the X-ray says the coffin bone is cracked, they need to rest this pony and take him out of work. Until then, we'll keep him in a stall in the barn with all our fingers firmly crossed.'

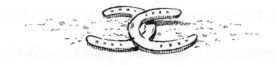

Next morning Jacob spoke to Marianne Forrester,

Cindy's mom, then put Nemo into the trailer and headed out to the large equine medical facility in Elk Springs where they would X-ray the Forresters' pony.

'We'll know one way or the other by lunchtime,' Allyson told Brooke and Keira. 'Meanwhile, we get on with our jobs.'

So Keira put her worries about Nemo to one side and went to fetch Stormcloud from the meadow. She approached him calmly and slipped the headstall on without a problem, led him quietly back to the corral and tethered him to a rail.

'You're so good,' she murmured as she used a brush to take the dust out of his coat, then ran a comb through his tangled mane and tail. When she'd finished, he didn't look like the same pony that she'd

first seen in the meadow at High Peak. Now his dappled coat gleamed and his mane was silky soft. Standing back to appreciate him, Keira even thought that he'd already started to put on weight.

'Quit admiring him and get to work!' Brooke quipped as she went into the tack room.

'She's right – we don't want you to get big-headed,' Keira grinned, untying Stormy and setting off across the corral with him.

Just then Brooke came back out. She carried Stormy's saddle, planning to sling it over a rail and attach a new cinch, ready for Keira to use when she was ready.

Maybe it was the sudden movement which Stormy caught out of the corner of his eye. Or maybe it was the sight of the hated saddle. Anyway, he reacted as if he was being attacked, rearing up and wrenching the lead rope out of Keira's hands.

Up he went, pawing the air like the bronco of old, thundering down, rearing again then bucking his way across the corral until he came to a barrier. Keira's heart pounded as she hoped he wasn't about to try and jump the gate.

'Sorry!' Brooke sighed, biting her lip and retreating into the tack room.

'It's OK – not your fault,' Keira told her. Stormy reared again, his hooves striking out at the gate, clattering against it as he dropped to the ground. The impact seemed to shock him even more and he set off at full gallop around the corral.

Keira waited. She knew that in the end he would run himself to a standstill. Until then there was no point trying to get near him.

But she watched with tears welling up as all her work faded before her eyes. Stormcloud was back to his crazy old rodeo self – a wild bucking bronco that no one would ever ride.

CHAPTER SEVEN

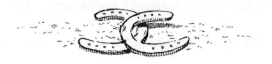

All that day Keira moped around the house worrying about Stormy.

'Back to square one, huh?' her mom asked kindly, kicking off her dusty old boots and leaving them on the porch. It was early evening and she'd just finished her work with Captain. They were still waiting for the results from Nemo's X-ray.

Keira sighed. 'I don't know if Stormy will ever stop spooking and going into his bucking bronco routine. The least little thing sets him off.'

Allyson paused beside Keira's chair. 'Nobody ever said it would be easy,' she reminded her. 'Take a while to think about it. What was the difference between yesterday, when it went well, and today, when it fell apart?'

'Yesterday we were out in the meadow, today we were in the corral.' Keira checked items off on her fingers. 'Yesterday, we worked alongside Red Star, today I left him behind . . . that's it!' Suddenly she could see a way forward. 'Red Star is good for Stormy – he keeps him calm and shows him what to do!'

'Good thinking,' her mom said, taking off her Stetson and going upstairs to shower.

Brooke had overheard the conversation and

came in from the porch. 'So you're not about to give up on Stormy?' she asked.

'No way. Tomorrow I bring them both out of the meadow – Stormy and Red Star. Me and my pony, from now on we're a team – we train ponies together!'

'Cool.' Brooke grinned then yawned. It had been a long day and their dad still wasn't home with Nemo. 'So what will you do with the money when you find a buyer for Stormy?'

'Whoa!' Keira laughed at the way Brooke's thoughts ran away with her. But then she decided to let her sister in on a secret that she was keeping from their mom and dad. 'Come up to my room!' she whispered.

Sneaking past the bathroom where the shower

was still running, Brooke followed Keira into her bedroom where their mom's latest copy of Western magazine lay open on her bed. Keira smoothed down the pages and pointed to a large ad.

'"Quality. Fit. Style."' Brooke read out loud. '"Exclusive since 1893."' She whistled in admiration at the pair of two-tone tan boots on display. 'Wow, you'll look cool in those!' she said.

Keira took the magazine from Brooke. 'Which colour do you like best? They make them in red and cream, turquoise and purple, or tan and beige.'

'Red and cream,'

Brooke decided. 'But I guess you could go for the tan and beige – they're classic colours.'

Keira grinned and hugged the magazine to her chest. She wrinkled her nose and finally let Brooke into the secret. 'They're not for me!'

'Then who?' Brooke asked with a puzzled frown.

'Which colour goes best with a dark bay horse – the red and cream or the two-tone tan?'

'Dark bay? You mean Captain?' Brooke said slowly.

Keira held her finger to her lips. 'Sshh! Yeah, these boots are for Mom when she rides in the competition at Elk Springs. But don't tell her.'

'I won't!' Brooke promised, her eyes sparkling.

''Cos I'll kill you if you do!' Keira hissed, closing the magazine and sneaking it back downstairs before Allyson finished her shower.

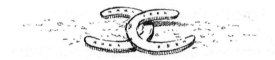

Just before the girls went to bed, Jacob drove the trailer back into the yard. Keira and Allyson went out to help him unload Nemo and even in the dusk light they could tell from his glum face that the news wasn't good.

'The coffin bone's broken, huh?' Allyson asked.

Carefully Keira unbolted the trailer ramp and let it down. She stepped inside, untied the Palomino and led him out.

'X-ray showed a definite crack,' Jacob confirmed. He was too tired and disappointed to say much, except that it was as they thought – poor Nemo would have to be rested for at least two months.

'Tough luck, little guy,' Keira murmured as she led him into the barn, down the centre aisle to a stall lined with fresh straw. 'You have to stay in here until Cindy comes to collect you. And no more competing, huh? Life's going to be pretty boring until you're healed.'

Nemo shuffled into the stall then turned and sighed. His head was down, his long blond forelock hanging low over his big brown eyes.

'Yeah!' Keira sighed with him as she bolted the door. 'Like Mom said – who said it would be easy where ponies are concerned?'

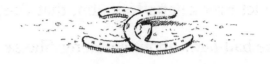

Thursday was a school day for Brooke and Keira. They hiked up the steep hill then stood at the end of their rough track where it joined the highway leading to Elk Springs, waiting for the yellow bus to come round the bend.

'Will Cindy Forrester be on the bus?' Brooke wondered, easing her bag of books from her shoulders and letting it rest on the ground.

'I guess,' Keira shrugged. 'But I don't know if Dad made the phone call yet.'

Neither of them looked forward to the conversation they would have with Nemo's owner if she already knew what had happened.

And it was obvious, as soon as the bus slowed down to let Brooke and Keira on, that Cindy had heard the bad news about her pony. She sat in the front seat, anxiously waiting to talk to them.

'Hey,' she mumbled. 'It's OK – Mom told me

about Nemo's foot, about the X-ray and everything. She says that you'll keep him at Black Pearl until Saturday, then we'll trailer him back to our place.'

'I'm real sorry,' Brooke said, sitting in the seat behind.

Keira sat next to Cindy, who was trying to put on a brave front but whose tanned face looked let down and worried. 'I'm sorry too,' she murmured. 'I was looking forward to being in the reining event, competing against you.'

'Yeah, Elk Springs is definitely off,' Cindy sighed, turning to stare out of the window. 'Mom says not to be too disappointed.'

Keira nodded and looked straight ahead. 'But you are?' she checked.

There was a long pause and another sigh before

Cindy answered in a broken voice. 'Yeah – I was totally looking forward to taking Nemo to the contest. Right now it feels like the end of the world.'

That day school dragged more than usual for Keira. All through maths and English she thought of the conversation she'd had with Cindy Forrester. *Imagine that was me and Red Star!* she thought. *I'd definitely feel like the world had ended.*

'Keira?' The maths teacher, Mr Solomon, broke her train of thought. 'Did you write down the homework I just gave you?'

But it gives us a good chance of winning at Elk Springs, Keira realised. *Cindy and Nemo would have*

been hard to beat. Without them in the competition,
maybe we'll get a prize.

'I said, run the spell check on this piece of work
before you print it out and hand it in,' the English
teacher, Mrs Ford, reminded Keira as she looked
over her shoulder at the computer screen. 'Did you
hear me, Keira, or are you in your own little
universe, dreaming about ponies as usual?'

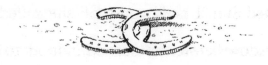

By the end of the day, Keira was dying to get home
and the journey on the school bus seemed to last
forever. Luckily, this time Cindy was sitting with
some buddies from her own class so Keira didn't
have to make awkward conversation.

'I won't be in school tomorrow,' Cindy told her

and Brooke as the bus driver stopped to drop them off. 'But we'll see you Saturday.'

'OK, see you!' Brooke and Keira waved from the roadside then they checked the mailbox, picked up three letters and set off along the Black Pearl track.

By the time they reached home, Keira had forgotten about Cindy and Nemo and was looking ahead to an hour in the round pen with Stormy. 'And Red Star, I need you too!' she called across the meadow before she dashed indoors to change into her sweatshirt and boots.

CHAPTER EIGHT

'Today is saddle day!' Keira announced to Red Star as she led him and Stormcloud out of the meadow.

Stormy snorted and high-stepped across the corral.

'That's right – you heard me – S-A-D-D-L-E!' Keira spelt it out as she tied the two ponies to a rail beside the tack room door. The two greys stood side by side, carefully watching as she stepped up into the porch then vanished inside.

She reappeared carrying Red Star's tack. 'Let's show Stormy how it's done,' she said calmly.

Red Star gave a nod and stood quietly as she slid the woven saddle pad across his back, smoothed it down then placed the saddle on top. Beside him, Stormcloud watched every move.

'OK, so we buckle the cinch – not too tight at first. Red Star knows it's not going to be a problem. We fasten a couple more straps around the neck and under the chest just like this and then we loop the latigo – the cinch strap – and slot it through this hole here nice and easy. That's it – that's all there is to it.'

Stormcloud still looked uneasy, though he seemed to be listening to Keira's soft, slow words.

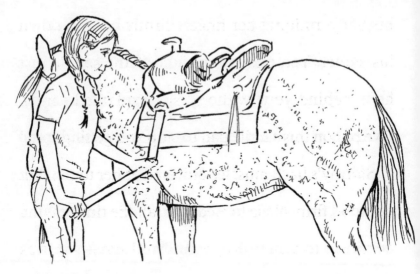

'I guess when you were a colt at the rodeo you didn't get any of that imprinting stuff Josh was telling me about,' she went on, turning away from Red Star and softly running her hand up and down Stormy's neck. 'It actually feels kind of nice to be stroked, doesn't it?'

Stormcloud breathed out through his nostrils, happy to let Keira pet him some more. She moved on from his neck to his back, feeling the warmth of his body, running her fingers firmly up and down his spine. 'You take the weight of the saddle just here, behind your withers,' she explained gently. 'We put on this saddle pad to stop you getting sore.'

Stormy's back muscles quivered at her touch, but he stood firm, close to Red Star, all the time paying attention to where Keira was and what she was about to do.

'Here at Black Pearl we care about stuff like saddle sores and making sure you're not hurting,' she assured him.

The next part was more difficult – she had to cross the porch again to go inside and fetch Stormy's saddle. 'Take care of him for me,' she told Red Star, who sidled up even closer to his nervous buddy.

Keira came back out. 'This here is nothing to be scared of,' she murmured, letting Stormcloud sniff at his saddle before she eased in between the two ponies and slid it on to his back.

He shifted a little, turned his head to look, then stood patiently as she drew the cinch under his belly and buckled it.

'See!' she breathed, smoothly running her hand up his neck and scratching behind his ears. 'With Red Star looking out for you, there's not a thing to worry about, believe me!'

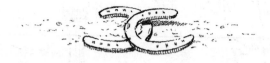

'I can't say it often enough – it's all about getting a horse or a pony to love you.' Jacob repeated his favourite mantra as he and Keira stood at the gate

to the round pen later that evening. They were watching Allyson train Captain in readiness for Elk Springs.

Allyson's graceful horse could spin on a dime and break from a standing start clean into a gallop across the arena. Then Allyson would rein him back and bring him to a halt within centimetres of the fence.

'Captain trusts your mom with his whole heart. That's the secret to this horse whispering thing they all talk about.'

'I know it,' Keira said quietly, thinking of the challenges that still lay ahead with Stormcloud. She told her dad how she'd got a saddle on him with Red Star's help.

'It makes it harder if the pony comes here with

a history,' Jacob admitted. 'Trust is harder to build up. But you knew that from the day you started.'

Keira nodded. 'One day Stormy will be winning prizes just like Captain,' she insisted, sighing as Allyson galloped close to where they stood.

Her mom wasn't wearing a hat and her reddish blonde hair blew free. The steel studs on her chaps glinted in the evening sun. But when Keira caught sight of her dusty old Cuban-heeled boots, she just sighed.

Jacob smiled. 'And one day you'll be a county reining champion like your mom!' he said, putting his arm around Keira's shoulders and walking her into the house.

Red Star was at Stormy's side again the next day when Keira led the rodeo pony into the round pen.

'Give me five minutes to bring Ruby in from the meadow,' Brooke called as she ran across the corral. 'Then I can ride Red Star for you while you work with Stormcloud.'

'Why is Ruby in the barn?' Keira asked when Brooke reappeared. Today there were low clouds hanging over the Black Pearl range and no shadows in the round pen, no sunset to the west.

'Mom says it's time for her to foal,' Brooke explained, stepping smoothly into the stirrup and sitting deep in Red Star's saddle. 'It could happen any day now. I put her in the stall next to Nemo.'

'How's he doing?' Keira asked as she stooped to pull Stormy's cinch a notch tighter.

'Poor little guy, he looks totally bored!' Brooke smiled wryly.

Keira stood up straight. 'OK, I'm about to do what Brooke just did with Red Star,' she told Stormy. 'I'm going to sit in the saddle and you're going to be happy about it. You're going to think, Hey, this could be fun – walking around the round pen with a rider on my back! No need for any bucking or rearing – no rodeo stuff here at Black Pearl Ranch, thank you!'

'Like he understands English!' Brooke grinned, setting off with Red Star at a slow walk.

'He does!' Keira insisted. She carried on talking to Stormy. 'See, my foot is in the stirrup and I'm swinging my leg over the saddle nice and easy.'

Stormcloud quivered. Keira could imagine

memories of the rodeo playing inside his head – the clash of the gates, the feel of sharp spurs on his flanks, the yell of the crowd as he exploded out of the narrow chute. But she sat in the saddle absolutely still and calm. He looked across the round pen and set off steadily to join Red Star.

'Nice and easy!' Keira breathed again. She held the reins loose and kept the pressure off Stormy's mouth. 'One step at a time.'

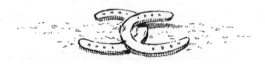

The weekend arrived and with it, the new farrier, Nathan Pearce, from the town of Sharman, named after the nearby lake. Keira was on the tack room porch, working through the list of chores her mom had given her. She'd already lined up Red Star for new shoes, and had also decided that it would be good experience for Stormy to stand alongside him as the farrier worked.

Nathan parked his white truck close to the barn door. The slam of his door as he stepped out startled Stormy, who tugged at his rope until Red Star nuzzled at his neck and told him to quit.

'Good boy, Red Star,' Keira told him. 'You see this, Stormy? Red Star is getting shiny new shoes!'

The burly farrier winked at Jacob, who had just brought Misty out of the meadow. Nathan was a big, middle-aged guy with a bald head and a long grey moustache. He wore a heavy leather belt with holsters for the tools of his trade – a hammer, a hoof pick, a pair of pliers. 'You want me to put shoes on all three?' he asked.

'Why not?' Jacob hadn't planned to have Stormy shod, but he looked chilled enough standing next to Red Star so he gave Nathan the go-ahead.

'Red Star first, please,' Keira said. And she talked Stormy through the whole thing – pulling out the nails of the worn shoes, hammering and shaping the new ones, the lifting of hooves and fixing into place.

They were so busy in the corral no one noticed the Forresters' trailer pull up by the house until Marianne Forrester walked towards them calling Jacob's name.

'We came for Nemo,' Cindy's mom reminded him, crossing the corral with Cindy close behind. Marianne wore her dark hair straight down her back, with a fringed leather jacket, three-quarter length denim skirt and fancy cowboy boots. Cindy was dressed the same, except for jeans with a silver belt buckle instead of a skirt. They looked the typical western mom and daughter – the well-heeled kind Keira recognised from the big county shows.

Her dad told her to fetch the Palomino and she ran quickly into the barn. She brought Nemo out slowly and carefully, to hear her dad telling the Forresters how sorry he was that Cindy's pony had cracked his coffin bone.

'That's not your fault,' Marianne said evenly, taking the rope from Keira and handing it to Cindy who led Nemo towards the trailer. 'It can happen any time to any pony.'

'You bring him back as soon as he's healed,'

Jacob insisted. 'And you don't pay me a cent until the job is done.'

'That's good of you.' Marianne thanked him but insisted on paying him for his work so far. Then they watched Cindy lead Nemo into the trailer. He went in without a hitch. 'Cindy feels pretty low,' Marianne confessed. 'Yesterday I actually took her around a few sale barns looking at possible replacements for Nemo.'

'I guess she wants a pony for Elk Springs. Did you see anything you liked?' Jacob asked.

Nathan had finished shoeing Red Star so he untied Stormy and handed him to Keira for her to hold while the farrier worked.

'She does,' Marianne reported. 'But you know Cindy – she has to fall totally in love with a pony before she'll compete with him. And I'm afraid nothing sparked her interest.'

'Stand!' Keira whispered in Stormcloud's ear as Nathan lifted a back hoof to scrape out the dirt. 'Nice and easy!'

Stormy tossed his head and swished his tail but with Keira at his head and Red Star at his side, he did as he was told. And he let Nathan take out the clippers and trim his hooves as the visitors watched.

'He's pretty,' Marianne Forrester murmured. She had a good eye and appreciated the proud angle of Stormy's head, the arch of his neck.

'Keira is training this pony,' Jacob told Marianne. 'My brother bought him from a rodeo outfit, so he's quite a challenge.'

'But he's good looking, isn't he, Cindy?'

Cindy glanced at Stormcloud. 'Yep,' she muttered with a frown, tugging at her mother's shirt sleeve. 'Nemo's waiting for us in the trailer. Come on, Mom, let's go!'

CHAPTER NINE

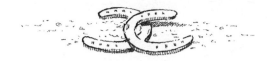

Next day, Sunday, Keira and Allyson were up early, working Red Star and Captain in the round pen. Both knew that, with only a week to go before the competition at Elk Springs, every second of training was vital, so the spins and flying lead changes were happening fast and furious in the enclosed space.

'How's Red Star doing with his new shoes?' Jacob asked Keira. He was going to the barn to check on Ruby but he paused to watch his wife and daughter hard at work.

'Pretty good,' she called back. 'I want to go through his routine one more time then I'll get on to my chores.'

'Take your time – no problem.' Resting his arms along the top fence rail, Jacob took a break. 'Captain put in one step too many on that sliding stop,' he informed Allyson as her dark bay horse skidded to a halt.

'I know it,' she sighed. She reined him to the right. 'Come on, buddy – let's get this sorted. We'll do it one more time.'

'But they're both looking good,' Jacob insisted, taking in every move with his expert eye. For another minute he watched them trot and lope, turn and spin – two riders in perfect harmony with their horses. Jacob grinned as he turned towards the barn. 'I reckon you two are just about ready to take on the world!' he laughed as he strode away.

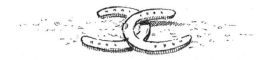

It was late morning before Keira had worked through her chores and was able to get to the next highlight of her day.

'Come on, Stormy,' she said as she fetched him from the meadow. She'd walked out there with Josh, who was visiting again with his dad, and the plan was for Josh to ride Red Star out along the Jeep trail while Keira rode Stormcloud.

'I'll believe it when I see it.' Josh had claimed that the wild bucking bronco he'd handed over a week earlier couldn't possibly be ready for trail riding. He'd frowned hard at Keira. 'I hope you know what you're doing.'

'Sure we do,' she'd replied, and now they were about to test it out. 'Let's go, Stormy,' she said, leading Josh and Red Star into the corral. Soon they had saddles on their ponies and were heading out by the creek.

'So this is the first time Stormcloud has been out of the round pen?' Josh was already impressed. Stormy wasn't acting up as they walked past the hay bales stacked by the barn door or spooking at the blue jays perched in the overhanging branches. In fact, his head was up and he was enjoying himself. 'What's your secret, Keira?'

'Red Star!' she grinned, leaning sideways to tug affectionately at her pony's ear. 'He's my secret weapon!' And she described to her cousin how they'd worked as a team.

Red Star broke into a proud trot ahead of Keira and Stormy. *I'll lead – you follow!*

'Cool.' Josh gave Red Star his head.

'Very cool!' Keira agreed.

The sun was high in the sky, the silvery leaves of

the willow bushes shimmered in the breeze and Stormcloud was trotting happily after Red Star, enjoying every moment.

They rode as far as the cattle guard separating Black Pearl land from the Reeds' property at the Three Horseshoes, then they turned around and headed for home. It was going on for two o'clock and from a distance Keira spotted more visitors arriving at the house.

'That looks like the Forresters' trailer,' she muttered. 'I don't get it. How come they brought Nemo back so soon?'

Josh and Keira picked up speed, trotting Red Star and Stormy along the last stretch of the trail and reaching the corral just as Marianne and Cindy came out of the tack room with Jacob.

'Surprised?' Marianne asked Keira, who carefully tethered Stormy to the nearest rail.

'Yeah. Where's Nemo?'

'He's back home, resting that foot.' Marianne Forrester seemed to be taking a close interest in Stormy, as she had done the day before. Once again, Cindy was hanging back. 'We came to chat with your dad about something else, but he tells me that you're the person we should be talking to.'

Keira was about to unbuckle Stormy's cinch. Instead she cocked her head to one side and let Cindy's mom continue.

'Cindy and I have been discussing a possible option,' she said, drawing her daughter forward. 'Go ahead, honey – explain.'

Cindy cleared her throat. 'Tell me no if it's a

problem,' she began awkwardly, her face flushed. 'But Mom and I – we both really like the look of Stormcloud.'

'Yeah, he's totally amazing,' Keira agreed. Still she didn't tune in to what the Forresters had in mind. 'You wouldn't have thought it when he first came here, when his head was all over the place because of what they put him through at the rodeo, but he's a smart guy.'

'Your dad says you've trained him real fast.'

'Red Star helped. Besides, Stormy's a quick learner.'

'And right now I don't have a pony I can ride . . .'

'Yeah, I know. That sucks.'

'So I – Mom and me – we were wondering if you would consider selling Stormcloud.'

Keira opened her eyes wide. Her eyebrows shot up towards her hairline. 'To you?' she yelped.

'Yeah, to us,' Cindy stammered, blushing like crazy. 'I'd really like to own him. What do you say?'

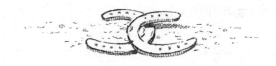

While Josh unsaddled Red Star and took him out to the meadow, Keira gave Cindy instructions on how to test-ride Stormcloud.

'You take it easy with him. He's young and still soft in the mouth, so don't yank his head around too much. He neck reins real easy. And just a touch with your legs – not too much.'

'I hear you.' As Cindy eased herself into the saddle, she spoke softly to Stormy. 'Easy does it.

You don't know me yet, but I'm not going to hurt you. I just want you to walk around the round pen with me on board. Is that OK?'

Keira watched her like a hawk. *Cindy talks sweetly to him – Stormy will like that,* she thought. *And her hands are nice and light – all good so far!*

But how would Stormy react when Cindy got him into the round pen without Red Star? Keira held her breath.

'Easy, easy,' Cindy whispered. Stormy hesitated at the gate to the pen and looked around for his buddy. He found himself alone with a new rider, skittered sideways and gave a little crow hop.

Don't go bucking Cindy off! Keira pleaded silently.

But his rider sat calm and steady, easing Stormcloud on with her legs. She coaxed him into a trot and took him around the outer edge of the arena.

'She's looking good,' Josh told Keira quietly. He was back from the meadow, standing next to Keira and watching the action.

'What a hero he is!' Keira sighed as Stormy went from trot to lope at Cindy's command. 'What a star!'

Cindy loped around the pen. She asked Stormy for a lead change – he obliged. A spin dead in the centre of the pen – another neat manoeuvre. A sliding stop – again, perfect.

'I totally love him,' Cindy told her mom, grinning broadly as she and Stormy loped by for the tenth time.

Marianne turned to Keira, her hand outstretched. 'We'll take him!' she said.

'Cool!' Before Keira knew it, she and Mrs Forrester were shaking hands. The deal was done.

'You know what this means?' Brooke asked Keira later that night.

Keira had stashed the cash that Marianne Forrester had given her for Stormcloud and was in

her room, poring over the ad in Western magazine. 'Yeah – it means I can buy Mom these boots!' she grinned.

She thought back to earlier in the afternoon when Cindy and Marianne had loaded Stormy into their trailer and they'd waved them off up the track. It had been a wrench to say goodbye – a real tug at her heart to see Stormy's cute head poking out of the back of the trailer, hearing him whinny as the Forresters drove away. 'I hope Stormy doesn't get homesick for Black Pearl Ranch,' she sighed.

'He won't. He'll like the Forresters' place – they're good people. Anyway, you don't get it,' Brooke insisted, sitting on Keira's bed and firmly closing the magazine. 'I mean, think about what this really means.'

'Boots for Mom – in time for Elk Springs!'

'No, forget the boots.' Brooke saw she had to spell it out. 'Cindy has a great new pony, thanks to you.'

Keira nodded. She went to the drawer where she'd put the money, took it out and counted it carefully. Enough for the boots and maybe a new saddle pad for Red Star.

'A new reining pony.' Brooke hammered out her point. 'She has a whole week to work with him before Elk Springs.'

'Oh!' Keira caught her breath and looked up at her sister.

'Exactly!' Brooke said, catching a twenty-dollar bill as Keira let it escape between her fingers and flutter to the ground. 'Next week at the reining competition – who will be your number one rival?'

'Stormy!' Keira breathed, getting it at last.

'Stormy,' Brooke repeated the name. 'And, according to Josh, the way Cindy rode him in the round pen this afternoon, those two could easily snatch first prize!'

CHAPTER TEN

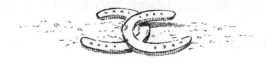

'This is so weird!' Keira said to Jacob as they drove into town.

There was a store on Main Street called Rocky Mountain Riders which sold the exact boots that Keira wanted for Allyson, so she'd confided in her dad and they'd arranged to make the trip on Wednesday while Allyson was out in Norton County giving a riding lesson to a client.

'What's weird about buying your mom a gift?' he

asked, turning down the country and western music and pointing out the entrance to Springs Stadium where the reining competition would be held in three days' time. 'She is going to be ecstatic.'

'No, not that.' Keira felt butterflies in her stomach at the thought of Saturday's upcoming event. 'I mean, it's weird that we'll be up against Stormcloud.'

'I hear you.' Jacob swung left at the lights on to Main Street and looked for a place to park the truck. 'You don't really want to compete against Stormy because you spent a lot of time with that pony and somehow he feels like family?'

'Totally,' she sighed. 'Part of me wishes I hadn't sold him to Cindy – and I don't mean because he might beat Red Star,' she added hastily.

Her dad nodded as he backed into a space close to Rocky Mountain Riders. 'All good trainers feel the same. We connect with the horses we work with and it's always hard to let them go.'

Somehow Keira felt better that her dad understood the problem. 'So it's not just me?'

'No way.' He got out and led the way into the store. 'Besides, Stormy is the first pony that you trained and sold – it's a big thing for you. A little way down the line you'll get more used to it.'

As they entered the shop the smell of new leather hit them. There were saddles and bridles, fancy chaps and chinks, Stetsons, spurs and lassos, all arranged neatly on shelves or hanging from hooks. Keira spotted the boots at the far end of the store and made a beeline towards them. She scanned the shelves and soon picked out the pair she wanted.

'I'd like the tan and beige burnished jersey-calf classics,' she told the young guy who stepped forward to help.

The assistant smiled at her certainty and took the boots from the shelf. 'You sure made up your mind ahead of time. Why don't you sit right down and try them on?'

Keira shook her head. 'They're not for me,' she said, taking the pointy-toed boots with their beautiful swirling stitched patterns and contrasting shades of tan leather. She turned them upside down to examine the tough soles and stacked heels. Then she raised them to her nose and breathed in the smell. To her mind they were the best boots money could buy. 'I'm giving them to my mom, Allyson Lucas, and I know she'll totally love them.'

The store assistant knew Allyson's name – he was a reining contest fan, though he only ever got to watch the event, never to compete. He took Keira's money, wrapped the boots and presented them to her with a wide smile, saying how lucky her mom was to have a daughter like her.

Keira blushed and thanked him. She walked out of the store with the box under her arm, feeling so proud she thought she would burst.

It was only when she was out on the sidewalk with her dad that she remembered about the saddle pad for Red Star so they retraced their steps and bought him a red, white and black blanket woven in traditional zigzags and stripes. The same assistant gave them a twenty per cent reduction and wished her luck for Saturday's competition.

'I'll be there in the crowd,' he promised. 'I'll be cheering for you and your mom to win!'

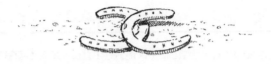

'When will you give Mom the boots?' an excited Brooke wanted to know.

It was late Wednesday evening and Keira had fitted in a training session with Red Star after she got back from town. Like Allyson always said – Practice makes perfect.

'Tonight, as soon as she gets back from Norton County,' Keira decided. 'That gives her two days to wear them in before the contest.'

'Good thinking. Hey, I hear her car!' Rushing out on to the porch, Brooke called for Keira to get ready.

Keira reached for the wrapped gift, almost tripping over Popcorn who was winding himself between her legs. He miaowed and shot out on to the porch ahead of her. Holding the box behind her back, Keira followed.

'What's this – a welcoming committee?' Allyson smiled at the girls as she crossed the yard. She waved hi to Jacob who was busy in the tack room porch, cutting leather for a new pair of chaps for their neighbour, Tom Walters – 'Heavy duty, nothing too fancy,' cattle rancher Tom had told him.

'Hi, Mom!' Brooke's voice bubbled with excitement. She picked up Popcorn and cuddled him close.

'Hi, Mom!' Keira echoed.

Allyson put her head to one side. 'What's up?'

'Nothing's up,' Brooke insisted.

'I bought you a gift,' Keira said shyly, feeling her heartbeat quicken and showing Allyson the box. 'You have to try them on for size.'

'A gift?' Her mom took the box, turned it this way and that.

'Open it!' Brooke urged.

So she carefully peeled back the sticky tape, slid her fingers under the wrapping and revealed the plain cardboard box. 'Is this what I think it is?' she murmured.

'Open it!' Brooke said again. Keira stood with her hands clasped to her chest, praying that her mom liked what she'd bought. *Maybe I should have chosen the purple and green*, she thought.

Allyson took the lid off the box and stared in wonder at the tan and beige beauties. She looked up at Keira and down at the boots, up at Keira again with tears in her eyes.

'Do you like them?' Keira whispered.

Without speaking Allyson kicked off her worn old boots and took the new ones from the box. She put them on, she paraded up and down the porch then she called Jacob to come and look. 'Like them?' she sighed. 'I totally love them!'

Then she hugged the breath out of Keira and they all shed tears of happiness, except Jacob, who

cleared his throat and said he had to look in on Ruby before it grew dark.

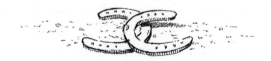

'My lucky boots!' Allyson swore that they would help her to win. She wore them from dawn to dusk through Thursday and Friday, taking Captain through his routine, perfecting every move.

'I think she likes them!' Keira told Red Star.

She too was in the round pen every spare moment – after school on Thursday and again on Friday, when she'd run into Cindy Forrester during lunch break and had a chance to ask her how Stormy had settled in.

'He's doing good,' Cindy had answered cagily. Like Keira, she was all too aware that Red Star and

Stormcloud were set to go head to head next day. 'The first night we got him home we put him in the stall next to Nemo. He's out in our meadow during the daytime and in the barn nights.'

'Cool.' How's he doing with his spins and sliding stops? Keira had wanted to ask, but she'd held back. After all, she would find out soon enough.

Keira had been ready to walk on down the corridor but Cindy had stopped her. 'Thanks for selling Stormy to me,' she'd said quietly so that no one else could hear. 'I guess you know he's a pony in a million.'

A lump had come into Keira's throat. 'I do,' she'd agreed. 'And I know that tomorrow he'll be hard to beat.'

So now, Friday evening, she spoke seriously to

Red Star as she returned him to the meadow after their final training session. 'Tomorrow is a big day,' she told him. 'I'll be out here before breakfast to bring you in for a special pamper session – shampoo and brush, hooves polished – the works. Then we load you into the trailer with Captain and we drive to Elk Springs.'

Red Star stood with her at the gate, resting his head on her shoulder, seeming to take in every word.

'We arrive at the stadium and we wait a couple of hours while the grown-ups compete – I know, waiting's the hard part. But Mom has the lucky boots I gave her and she swears she's going to win.'

Red Star blew through his lips – a soft burring sound.

'Then it's you and me.' Keira hooked her arm under his neck and ran her fingers through his mane. 'Up against your old buddy, Stormcloud.'

Red Star turned to nuzzle her cheek.

'I know,' she murmured, gazing up at the shadowy mountains. 'Cindy and Stormy make a good team.'

Not as good as us! Red Star suggested with a toss of his head. And he left Keira and loped across the darkening meadow, neck arched and tail streaming out behind him.

CHAPTER ELEVEN

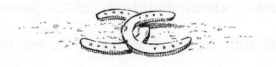

'**M**ay 1st – the start of the competition season here at Springs Stadium!' the voice on the tannoy system announced to a big crowd. There was a hum of excitement as the men's reining contest got underway, a rising wave of gasps as horses and riders misjudged their turns and sliding stops, cheers at every flying lead change and spin.

'Exciting, huh?' Keira said to Red Star in the

waiting area beside the stadium where dozens of trailers were parked. Though she hated the waiting, she loved the buzz of the big event.

It was ten-thirty and Allyson was already out in the practice arena, putting Captain through his paces. Brooke reported back that the two of them were looking good. 'Dad's in the competitors' stand, waiting for the women's event to begin,' she told Keira. 'Why don't you join him? I'll wait here with Red Star.'

So Keira quickly made her way into the stadium, threading through the crowd until she spotted her dad.

'The women's event is about to start,' he told her. 'Your mom's third in line.'

Keira watched each horse and rider enter the

arena, heard the cheers and gasps, waiting impatiently for her mom and Captain to appear.

'Here they come!' Jacob warned.

All heads turned to watch the next competitor enter. Allyson sat straight and easy, her long legs pressed gently against Captain's sides. Keira smiled as she noted her mom's white Stetson, crisp yellow

shirt, pressed blue jeans and those brilliant new boots. 'Let's hope they really are lucky,' she murmured.

A bell rang. Keira held her breath as Allyson began her routine.

She completed two circuits around the arena at a trot, breaking into a lope on the diagonal, then into a gallop around the rim, sliding to a halt under the judge's table. Still Keira hardly dared to breathe.

'Watching is ten times worse than doing a thing yourself,' Jacob muttered.

Keira nodded. Now Allyson and Captain were in the centre of the arena, spinning on the spot – first anti-clockwise, then clockwise, graceful and precise. With a small shift of her weight in the saddle, Allyson brought Captain out of the second spin into another gallop, skimming the edges of the arena, reining him sharply out of each corner.

One day I'll be this good, Keira promised herself.

Four minutes dead – Allyson and Captain finished their routine. The crowd exploded out of their tense silence into deafening applause.

'That was our local gal – Black Pearl's Allyson Lucas on Captain,' the announcer yelled above the noise. 'Next out is Melodie Clearman on her Appaloosa mare, Miss Candy!'

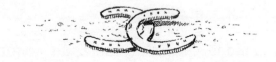

There was more waiting – five more competitors, each aiming to take home the prize money. Then the worst wait of all while the judges made their decision. Finally the result came over the tannoy.

'In third place in the women's reining contest is Melodie Clearman on Miss Candy. Second place goes to . . .

Keira crossed all her fingers, squeezed her eyes tight shut . . .

'Ann W. Harris on Nebraska Boy! And the winner of the first prize is . . .'

Please, please, please! Keira prayed.

'The gifted, polished and immaculate Allyson Lucas on Captain!'

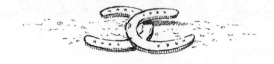

Her mom had won and somehow after this Keira didn't care so much if Red Star didn't manage to pull it off in the junior contest.

'Let's go in there and have a good time,' she told

him as she rode around the practice arena then lined up behind Cindy and Stormcloud.

Cindy turned to wish Keira luck.

'Likewise,' Keira told her with a warm smile. 'You knock the socks off those judges, you hear me, Stormy?'

The proud ex-rodeo pony went on into the big arena, head high, trotting right up to the judges' table where he waited for the start bell. There he stood, calm and confident, his dappled coat smooth and shining, his dark mane brushed to silky smoothness.

'Who'd have thought it?' a voice asked, and Keira glanced down to see Josh leaning on the fence. 'Am I watching a miracle, or what?'

'I know!' she sighed. Even she could hardly

believe that this was the pony her Uncle Kevin had
rescued from the sale barn.

'Go, Stormy!' Josh called as the bell rang and
Cindy urged him into a trot.

Trot-lope-sliding-stop. Spin-spin-lope-stop. Back
up for five steps turn-lope into flying lead change . . .
Stormcloud was near perfect. At the end of their
routine, Cindy lifted her hat to the judges and rode
out.

Keira raised her hand to high-five her rival. 'Cool routine,' she told Cindy as she trotted into the arena. She heard Josh yell, 'Go, Red Star!' then the crowd drowned him out and she heard nothing, saw no one, was aware only of the lights shining down on the arena and the bell signalling the start of their routine.

'Ready?' she murmured.

Red Star flicked his left ear and pawed the ground. *Totally ready. Let's go!*

At the end of the competition Cindy and Stormy stood next to Keira and Red Star, waiting for the judges' decision. The two ponies put their heads together and seemed to chat. *Cool routine . . . Next*

time, maybe tighten up the clockwise spin . . . Not bad for a beginner.

'Third spot in the girls' reining contest goes to Sarah Davis on Silent Spirit!' The announcement raised a cheer and Keira watched a girl with long fair braids ride her paint pony up to the judges' table to receive her prize.

Cindy cast a nervous glance at Keira then held up her hands to show how tight her fingers were crossed.

'Second prize was a close call, but the judges have awarded it to . . . newcomers Cindy Forrester and Stormcloud!'

Keira clapped and cheered as Stormy trotted up for his award. She raised her fist and saluted Cindy. First time out and he got second place. Who knew how far the rodeo pony could go and what brilliant highlights his future held!

'First place . . . impossible to fault . . .' Keira held her breath and tuned in to the announcement. 'It's our old favourite . . . they keep it in the family . . . Keira Lucas and Red Star!'

'Back to reality,' Jacob said next morning.

Dawn had just broken but Keira was already up and dressed, walking with her dad across the corral to the barn to see if Ruby had foaled overnight. A cold mist covered the ground and cloaked the peaks of the Black Pearl range.

'Still buzzing from yesterday?' he asked, opening the barn door and striding on down the aisle.

Keira nodded. The memories were fresh – receiving first prize, celebrating with Cindy and Stormy then trailering home with Red Star and Captain. She'd fallen into bed and was asleep before her head hit the pillow.

'It turned out great, huh?' Jacob reached Ruby's stall and peered inside. He smiled then invited Keira to take a look.

There in a bed of straw lay Ruby's newborn foal, a sorrel with a white flash down his nose, his mom standing guard over him.

'Can I go in?' Keira asked.

Jacob nodded and opened the stall door.

Kneeling down in the straw, Keira reached out her hand to stroke the defenceless foal. He was soft and warm. 'Hey, baby,' she murmured, running her hand down his neck, along his back and under his belly.

'Good job, Momma,' Jacob told Ruby after he saw that all was well. He smiled at Keira kneeling in the straw. 'If this is back to reality, it can't be bad, huh?'

'Totally cool,' she agreed.

She gazed at the foal and looked ahead into the future. In a year's time she would have this sorrel foal in the round pen, working him on a long line, training another champion . . .

Keira's home is **Black Pearl Ranch**, where she helps train ponies – and lives the dream …

Black Pearl Ponies

Red Star is the love of Keira's life and the best pony ever. But he's in danger: he's gone missing in the snowy mountains, home to bears and coyotes.

Has he escaped? Or has he been stolen? Either way, can Keira rescue her beloved pony in time?

Keira's home is **Black Pearl Ranch**, where she helps train ponies – and lives the dream …

Black Pearl Ponies

Reed Walters' new pony, **Wildflower**, is beautiful but untrained. Keira warns Reed not to push her too hard, but he insists on showing her off at the local rodeo.

Disaster strikes: Wildflower bolts from the arena. Keira and her sister head off into a snowstorm to find her, forgetting the one golden rule – always stick together …

Keira's home is **Black Pearl Ranch**, where she helps train ponies – and lives the dream …

Black Pearl Ponies

MISS MOLLY

Sable's parents plan to give her a surprise birthday gift – a sorrel mare called **Miss Molly!** They allow Keira's dad three short weeks to train the nervy pony.

Soon Sable is ready to meet Miss Molly, but it all goes horribly wrong. Why does the pony spook big-time? Keira turns detective to find out.

Keira's home is **Black Pearl Ranch**, where she helps train ponies – and lives the dream ...

Black Pearl Ponies

SNICKERS

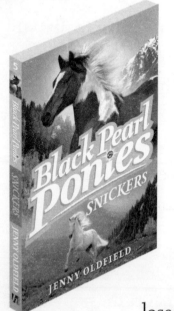

Keira is thrilled when two high bred ponies arrive at the ranch, but she soon falls out with the owner's spoiled son, Rex.

Rex breaks all the rules, but when he mistreats poor **Snickers** Keira faces a tough choice: confront Rex and lose valuable business, or keep quiet and risk Snickers coming to serious harm?